Perfectly POPPY

The Big Bike

story by Michele Jakubowski

pictures by Erica-Jane Waters

Curious

First published in the UK by Curious Fox,
an imprint of Capstone Global Library Limited,
7 Pilgrim Street, London, EC4V 6LB
Registered company number: 6695582

www.curious-fox.com

Illustrations by Erica-Jane Waters
All characters in this publication are fictitious and any resemblance to real persons,
living or dead, is purely coincidental.

ISBN 978 1 782 02200 8
19 18 17 16 15
10 9 8 7 6 5 4 3 2 1

A CIP catalogue for this book is available from the British Library.

Image credits: Shutterstock
Designer: Kristi Carlson

Printed in China by Nordica
0914/CA21401512

Table of Contents

Chapter 1

A New Bike

It was a big day for Poppy.

She was getting a new bike!

Poppy had worked very hard to

learn how to ride her old bike,

but it was too small now.

"I'm going to miss my old bike," Poppy told her best friend, Millie. "But my new bike will have a basket and a bell."

"That sounds really cool," Millie said.

"My dad is bringing it home after work," Poppy said.

"You are so lucky," Millie said.

"My mum
and dad said we
could take a bike
ride together
this weekend,"
Poppy said.

"Where would we go?"
Millie asked.

"They said we could take the
trail that leads all the way to the
park!" Poppy said.

"We never get to go that far!"
Millie said.

"I know! It is a long ride, so my mum said she'll pack us a picnic," Poppy said.

"You love food!" Millie said.

"And you love the park," Poppy said. "Now I just need my new bike."

Chapter 2

A Very Big Bike

After Millie left, Poppy couldn't wait for her dad to come home with her new bike. Finally, she saw his car pull into the driveway.

"My new bike is here!" she

shouted as she ran out the door.

Poppy's mum and older
brother, Nick, followed her
outside. They got there just as
Poppy's dad took her new bike
out of the car.

"Wow!" her mum said.

"That's awesome!" Nick said.

He never thought anything of
Poppy's was awesome.

But Poppy just stood there
with her mouth open.

Finally she said, "It's so big."

"It is big," her dad said. He
brought the bike over to Poppy.
"But you're a big girl now, so you
need a big bike."

Poppy looked at her old bike.

It was small and easy to ride. This

new bike looked scary.

"Get on, Poppy," her dad said.

"No, thank you," she said.

"Come on, Poppy," her mum
said. "Don't be scared."

"I'm not scared," said Poppy.

"I just like my old bike better."

"Really?" her dad asked.

"Really," Poppy told him.

"You can take this one back to

the shop."

"You don't even want to try

it?" her dad asked.

"Not really," Poppy said.

Poppy's mum put her arm around her shoulder.

"Don't worry, Poppy," she said. "You'll get used to this bike in no time."

Poppy wasn't so sure, but she did agree to keep the bike.

Chapter 3

The Best Bike

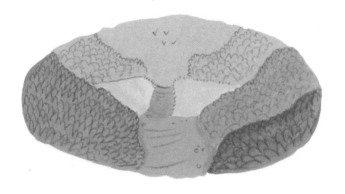

By Saturday, Poppy was still unsure about her new bike. She had ridden it on the driveway a few times. She hadn't fallen, but she was still scared.

The trail was long. She wasn't sure she could make it all the way to the park on her big bike.

Millie quickly
put on her elbow
pads, kneepads
and helmet. Poppy
put on her gear
very slowly.

"Let's go!" Millie said.

She hopped on her bike and
raced away. Nick and his friend
Thomas raced by, too.

"Come on, Poppy!" Nick said.
"We don't have all day."

"Just a minute," Poppy said.

She watched as Nick, Thomas and Millie sped down the trail without her. She didn't like being left behind.

Poppy took a deep breath and started pedalling. At first, she was shaky. Then she pedalled a little faster and felt better.

The faster she went, the more
confident she felt. By the time
they got to the park, Poppy felt
great. She loved her new bike!

"I can ride so much faster on my new bike," Poppy told Millie.

"Do you still miss your old bike?" Millie asked.

"Not at all!" Poppy said with a smile. "This bike is the best!"

Poppy's Diary

Dear Diary,

I got a new bike! When I first saw it, I was scared. It was so big! I missed my old bike. Getting used to something new can be hard.

Today we went for a ride to the park and it was so much fun. Once I tried it, my big bike wasn't scary. I can't wait to go out again on my new bike!

Poppy

Bike Fun and Games

I love biking around the area where I live, but I also love to play these bike games with Millie.

Bike challenge

Draw a wide chalk line down your driveway. You can make it straight, curvy or a figure of eight shape. You can even make a few different courses if you like. Take turns timing each other on the courses. See how fast and how slow you can go without stopping.

Bike wash

Instead of a car wash, have a bike wash! Grab a hose, a bucket, soap, a sponge and a towel and get scrubbing. You might even earn some money!

Bike horse

Pretend your bike is a horse. Give your horse a name, make a stable and be sure to ride and take care of it. Be creative and have fun!

Obstacle course

Using buckets, cones, skipping ropes and other items from your garage, create an obstacle course. See who can go the fastest and who can go the slowest without stopping.

Perfectly POPPY

The Big Bike £3.99
9781782022008

Poppy's Puppy £3.99
9781782021988

Football Star £3.99
9781782021995

Outside Surprise £3.99
9781782022015

Read all of Poppy's adventures!
Available from all good booksellers.